Disney's
Anytime
Stories
COLLECTION

A
MOUSE WORKS
STORYBOOK COLLECTION

"Bambi Makes Friends" is based on the original story,
Bambi, A Life in the Woods, by Felix Salten, published by Simon & Schuster.

"Dumbo Leads the Way" is based on the Walt Disney motion picture,
Dumbo, suggested by the story, *Dumbo, the Flying Elephant,*
by Helen Aberson and Harold Perl, ©1939 Rollabook Publishers, Inc.

"Watch Dogs," a *101 Dalmatians* story, is based on the book
by Dodie Smith, published by Viking Press.

Written by Lisa Ann Marsoli
Penciled by Orlando de la Paz, Denise Shimabukuro and Scott Tilley
Painted by Atelier Philippe Harchy, Orlando de la Paz, Adam Devaney,
John and Phillip Hom, Michael Humphries, Yakovetic and Kenny Yamada
Digital art by Thomas S. Phong
Designed by Deborah Boone
©1996 Disney Enterprises, Inc.
Printed and bound in the United States of America
ISBN 1-57082-408-8
10 9 8 7 6 5 4 3 2

Table of Contents

The Genie's Day Off   *Aladdin*   8

A Dream Come True   *The Little Mermaid*   12

Bambi Makes Friends   *Bambi*   16

The Magic Attic   *Sleeping Beauty*   20

A Busy Day of Play   *Beauty and the Beast*   24

True Friends   *Pinocchio*   28

Tod and Copper Act Up   *The Fox and the Hound*   32

Saved by the Cat   *Oliver & Company*   36

Dumbo Leads the Way   *Dumbo*   40

Cinderella's Uninvited Guests   *Cinderella*   44

Timon's Snack Attack   *The Lion King*   48

"Watch" Dogs   *101 Dalmatians*   52

Mowgli the Bear Tamer   *The Jungle Book*   56

The Genie's Day Off

The Genie had been working night and day. Aladdin wanted to win the hand of Princess Jasmine, but it was going to take some doing. The Genie had already transformed Aladdin into Prince Ali. Then he'd saved him from the bottom of the ocean. Now the Genie had to find a way to stop Jafar before he used his wicked ways to marry the princess.

"Listen, Aladdin," the Genie said. "I love my work, I really do, but I need a day off. I need time to recharge the batteries, get the ol' magic back on the job, if you know what I mean."

"Your wish is my command," laughed Aladdin. "After all, you've earned it."

"You're the best boss a genie ever had!" shouted the Genie. Then he disappeared back into the lamp for a nice long nap.

Meanwhile, Aladdin was strolling through the marketplace, Abu on his shoulder and the lamp tucked under his arm. Suddenly there was a great buzz of excitement as a caravan of elephants paraded down the narrow street.

Abu was munching peanuts when one of the elephants decided to help himself to some. Aladdin was pushed out of the way by the hungry pachyderm. He landed on a pile of pillows, still holding onto the lamp. The elephant thought there might be something tasty in the lamp. Grabbing hold of it with his trunk, he flung the lamp into the air when he didn't find anything to eat.

"Oh, no! Abu, quick! Go after it!" yelled Aladdin. But it was too late, for the lamp sailed out of sight within seconds. Inside, the Genie dreamed he was flying through a clear blue sky, heading for a tropical paradise filled with swaying palm trees and big glasses of pineapple juice with little paper umbrellas in them. THUD! The lamp landed in an alley on the other side of the bazaar. A short while later, a fierce storm kicked up and swirled through the alley.

A gust of wind picked up the lamp and bumped it along the road. PING! PING! PING!

"I've been in paper bags with walls thicker than this!" complained the Genie.

Finally the wind died down and the lamp came to rest outside a stable. "Peace and quiet at last!" sighed the Genie with relief as he climbed into a nice, warm bubble bath.

Outside the lamp, a merchant was trying to persuade his stubborn donkey to accompany him to market. The man pulled and pulled on the rope, but the donkey wouldn't budge. When the animal got fed up, it struck out with its back legs, sending the lamp high above Agrabah.

Moments later, the lamp came to rest in Aladdin's rooftop home. Aladdin arrived home just as the lamp dropped in, safe and sound.

When the Genie emerged from the lamp, covered in suds, he cracked his neck. "Wow, that smarts!" he cried.

"Why don't you take another day off," suggested Aladdin. "You look awful!"

"Please!" pleaded the exhausted Genie. "If I relax any more, it will kill me!"

A Dream Come True

It was another beautiful day under the sea, and Ariel and Flounder were out in search of adventure. "C'mon, Flounder, catch up!" cried Ariel as she dove in and out of the clear, blue water.

"Sorry, Ariel, I'm kind of tired. I haven't been sleeping very well," Flounder yawned.

Suddenly something caught Ariel's eye in the distance. "Look, Flounder—a sunken ship!" the Little Mermaid called.

"A sunken ship?" Flounder echoed with a gulp.

The two friends swam up to the old wooden ship that was half-buried in the sand.

"I'll bet there are some wonderful human things inside for my collection," Ariel said. "C'mon! Follow me!"

Flounder hurried to catch up. But instead of finding Ariel inside the ship, he was met by a small shark with big, sharp teeth.

"Help! Ariel! Help!" Flounder called. He turned and darted back out of the ship. Within seconds, Ariel came rushing out, too.

"What's the matter, Flounder?" she asked. "Are you all right?"

When Flounder explained what had happened, Ariel decided they'd had enough adventure for one day. "Let's get a good night's sleep and come back tomorrow," she suggested.

That night, Flounder dreamed of a hundred different creatures, all with huge, pointy white teeth and cold black eyes. In the morning, he was still not ready to return to the ship with Ariel.

"I know," said Ariel. "The next time you have that dream, imagine the creatures' teeth are really made of fluffy white clouds. Everyone knows a fluffy white cloud can't hurt you."

"I'll try," Flounder promised. But when Flounder took his nap that afternoon, he had another dream. This one was about a scary-looking sea monster with long white whiskers poking out from its pointy snout.

"Oh, dear!" Ariel exclaimed when Flounder described his latest nightmare. "That monster sure sounds awful. But since he has long white whiskers, why don't you try imagining that he's a kind, grandfatherly monster."

"Thanks, Ariel," said Flounder. "I'll try anything! All these bad dreams are making me tired!"

That night, Flounder closed his eyes. The moment he drifted off, he dreamed of swimming into a dark tunnel. But it wasn't really a tunnel—it was the open mouth of a huge gray whale. Flounder took a deep breath. He knew exactly what to do to turn this bad dream around! The little fish quickly found a way out through the whale's blowhole. Sure enough, as soon as the whale spouted water, Flounder came riding out on top.

The next morning, Flounder proudly told Ariel what he had done.

"That's wonderful," said Ariel. "Now maybe you can help me with a nightmare I had last night. In it, I saw a handsome prince on board a ship, but I couldn't be with him because he was a human and I was a mermaid."

Flounder thought for a moment. "I know," he said. "The next time, why don't you just dream that you become human, too?"

Ariel smiled. "That's a good idea, Flounder," she said. Then she let out a long sigh. "If only dreams came true!" she added wistfully.

Bambi Makes Friends

Bambi nestled close to his mother. He was a shy little fawn, and the woods that surrounded him seemed vast and strange. But now that Bambi was getting older, it was time that he learned about his home. One day he would be Prince of the Forest, and he would need to know and respect all its creatures. Fortunately, there was one animal who was more than eager to show it to him.

"Hiya, Bambi!" Thumper called as he hopped through the grass. "Wanna come for a walk?"

"He'd love to. Thank you, Thumper," replied Bambi's mother before Bambi could say a word. She gently nudged her fawn to his feet.

"But I'd rather stay here with you," Bambi replied nervously.

"You'll be fine," his mom reassured him. "Thumper will take good care of you. Won't you, Thumper?"

"Sure will!" exclaimed Thumper. "Let's go!"

Bambi's eyes grew wide as he hesitantly followed Thumper deeper into the forest.

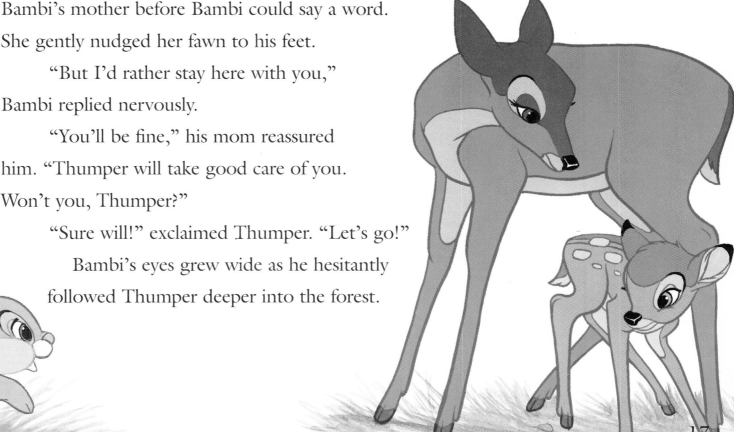

He was surrounded by so many creatures he'd never seen up close before. So those were the owls whose hoots he heard in the night! And there were the skunks whose scent he'd smelled when danger had threatened them! But by far the most amazing sight was a family of opossums who were hanging upside-down from a tree limb by their tails.

"Can you teach me how to do that, too?" Bambi asked Thumper.

Thumper giggled. "No, silly!" he replied. "Opossums can hang by their tails, but rabbits and deer can't. Every creature in the forest is different."

Just then they were distracted by the frantic chirping of a mother bird up ahead. When they asked her what was wrong, she told them that one of her babies was missing. Thumper and Bambi joined in the search, looking under bushes and behind trees. Then Bambi heard a PEEP PEEP coming from inside a hollow log.

"Oh, thank you!" said the mother bird gratefully when she was reunited with her baby.

Next, down by the stream, they came upon a busy beaver.

"Wannna play?" asked Thumper.

"I can't," the beaver replied. "I'm building a dam."

"It would go faster with three of us," Bambi suggested. The beaver agreed, and soon Bambi was gathering sticks while Thumper helped the beaver pat everything into place. The dam was done in no time, and they all stood back to admire it.

"Now, that's what I call teamwork!" said the happy beaver. Then the three enjoyed a spirited game of tag.

When Thumper brought Bambi home late that afternoon, his mother was there waiting.

"Hello, dear," she said. "How was your walk with Thumper?"

Bambi's words came out in a tumble. He described everything he had seen and done with great excitement.

Bambi's mother smiled. She knew that one day Bambi would make a fine Prince of the Forest.

The Magic Attic

Briar Rose lived with three kindly old women in a cottage in the forest. They had raised her since she was a baby, and Briar Rose loved them very much. But Flora, Fauna, and Merryweather, as they were called, had a secret. They were actually fairies with magical powers, though they had vowed not to use them as long as Briar Rose was under their care.

One morning the three women set out to do some chores, leaving Briar Rose alone with her mending. "Oh, dear," she said to herself as she inspected a ripped apron. "This tear is worse than I thought!" But then Briar Rose remembered some old cloth in the attic.

"I could use it to make some patches," she thought as she climbed the stairs.

"What a mess!" she cried when she opened the attic door. "I'll never find what I'm looking for in here!" She began lifting the sheets off the furniture and poking in boxes. But there was one box she didn't see.

In it were the three magic wands Flora, Fauna, and Merryweather had put there for safekeeping many years ago. Ever since then, the magic within the wands had been just twitching to get out!

Briar Rose sifted through the contents of a drawer and discovered an old dress pattern. "How I wish I had some pretty silk!" she said wistfully. "I'd make those dear ladies some fancy new dresses." Hearing this, Flora's wand began to dance inside its box. Soon it went flitting across the room to just a few feet from where Briar Rose stood. Instantly, an old bolt of fabric propped against the wall transformed into cascades of fine pink silk.

"I can't believe it!" Briar Rose exclaimed when she discovered the cloth. "Now, what can I use for the sashes?"

Fauna's wand sprung into action, swirling behind Briar Rose. Briar Rose turned and spotted the spool of pale yellow ribbon that was now on the table.

"I know that wasn't there before!" she exclaimed. She tucked the ribbon under her arm and headed for the stairs.

Just then, Merryweather's wand knocked over a basket. When Briar Rose turned toward the sound, the wand flew over to the stairs and left a wooden box filled with delicate, tiny buttons in its wake. "My, this is my lucky day!" Briar Rose cried.

When the fairies returned home later that afternoon, Briar Rose was busy cutting, pinning, and stitching. She explained everything that had happened in the attic, telling them, "It was as if it all appeared by magic!"

"Magic!" cried Flora, acting shocked.

"Dear child, you mustn't fill your head with such nonsense," chided Fauna with mock concern.

Merryweather mounted the steps to the attic, and turned to the other two fairies. "Why don't you give me a hand up here," she said.

"Yes, that place does need a good cleaning," agreed Briar Rose, rising to help. But the fairies assured her they could handle the job on their own. By nightfall the attic was clean, with everything in its place, including three mischievous wands locked tightly in a little trunk—at least for the time being!

A Busy Day of Play

Mrs. Potts bustled about the castle as she did every morning, going over a list of all that needed to be done. "First of all, tidy the dining room," she said. "And the kitchen is a frightful mess. Yes, we'll need to sweep and scrub and…" She was suddenly interrupted by her son Chip.

"Hi, Mom!" he called brightly. "What are we going to do today?"

"Well, Chip, I'm not sure. There's so much I have to attend to," answered Mrs. Potts. "But I promise to call you the minute my work is finished."

"All right," Chip said softly. Disappointed, he wandered into the library and discovered Belle curled up in a cozy armchair, reading a book.

"Belle," Chip began, "why do grown-ups have to work all the time?"

Belle thought for a moment. "Well, they don't always have to," she said, "though sometimes it may seem that way. Why?"

"Because whenever I want to play with my mom, she's too busy," Chip explained.

Outside in the hall, Mrs. Potts overheard their conversation. It was clear that Chip missed her, and she missed him too. Still, everyone depended on her to keep the castle running smoothly. How would she find more time to be with Chip? Then Mrs. Potts got a wonderful idea.

"Chip!" she called from the library door. "How would you like to help with the chores? The faster we get done, the faster we can play!"

"Boy, would I!" Chip chirped. "See you later, Belle!" he called as he hopped happily after his mother.

"First we need to get that china closet straightened up," said Mrs. Potts. "Why don't we make up a rhyme to let everyone know what to do?"

"Let me try!" Chip begged. He thought for a moment, then sang out, "Cups and saucers, find your mate. Take your place and stand up straight!"

Mrs. Potts laughed with delight as the china flew into action and stood in pairs, all in a line.

"Now, on to the kitchen!" she exclaimed.

Mrs. Potts called to the featherduster. "Time to take a little spin." She winked at Chip and gave him a nudge. "Hop on!" The little teacup climbed aboard and the featherduster took off across the floor, gliding and swirling.

"Now it's time to take care of the dishes." Mrs. Potts said.

She filled the sink and made sure that every dish took a dip in the warm, soapy water. When the last plate was washed, she said, "You know, Chip, I think you could do with a bath yourself." Chip jumped into the water. He splashed and splashed, sending bubbles floating across the kitchen.

"Gee, Mom," said Chip, giggling. "I thought you worked all day—but now I know the truth. All you really do is play!"

"We're two of a kind," laughed Mrs. Potts, winking at Chip.

27

True Friends

Pinocchio couldn't believe it! He was off to his first day of school, just like any other boy. Pinocchio so looked forward to meeting the children and making new friends! He tucked his books under his arm and bid goodbye to Geppetto, who stood watching proudly from the doorstep. Jiminy Cricket was supposed to go, too, but he was still fast asleep. Pinocchio ran to catch up with the children who were already heading down the lane.

"Hello," said Pinocchio shyly to the other boys and girls. He knew he must have appeared strange to them. "Would it be all right if I walked with you to school?" he asked. Pinocchio held his breath, hoping desperately that the children would say yes.

The children looked at him curiously for a moment. Finally, a boy spoke up. "Sure, you can walk to school with us," he told Pinocchio.

"You can even be our friend. But there's something you have to do first. Come on!" Then he took off running. Pinocchio was so pleased—he was willing to do anything the boy asked. Pinocchio and the other children followed until the boy stopped in front of a bakery. "There's always a plate of cookies on the counter inside," the boy said. "All you have to do is go inside and get some for us." The other children watched Pinocchio closely, wondering what he would do.

Pinocchio knew in his heart that taking things that didn't belong to him was wrong. But he wanted the children to like him more than anything. "All right," he said. He gathered his courage, slipped into the shop, and grabbed a handful of warm oatmeal cookies. But as he dashed for the door, Pinocchio tripped and went sprawling into a bakery case. Cakes crushed beneath him, and loaves of bread went skidding across the floor. Hearing the noise, the old baker appeared from the back room. "What on earth?" he murmured.

Pinocchio panicked and pointed out the door.

"One of *them* did it!" he lied. But the street was empty except for the tiny figure of Jiminy Cricket.

"Your nose is growing, Pinocchio," remarked the cricket. "Have you forgotten your promise to tell the truth so quickly?"

"I guess I wanted to be friends with the other boys and girls too much," admitted Pinocchio. "I won't do it again."

Then he looked back at the baker. The kindly old man reminded him of Geppetto. Pinocchio began to clean up the mess. "I'm sorry I wrecked your shop," Pinocchio said. "I'll come back after school and help you make new cakes and bread to replace the ones I've ruined. I promise."

The baker smiled gratefully. He could see that Pinocchio was truly sorry. "Maybe we'll even have a few oatmeal cookies while we work!" he chuckled. Then he waved as Pinocchio and Jiminy Cricket headed out the door. "I guess I made a new friend today, after all," Pinocchio remarked.

"Isn't that the truth!" exclaimed Jiminy Cricket, proud that Pinocchio was indeed on his way to becoming a real boy.

Tod and Copper Act Up

Unlikely as it was, Tod the fox and Copper the pup were the best of friends. Because Copper was a hunting dog, he was supposed to go after foxes like Tod. And Tod, like any smart fox, should have been afraid of Copper. But when the two first met, they didn't know what was expected of them. The pup and fox innocently played in the woods together. Not that Tod was any ordinary fox. Orphaned when he was a newborn, he had been adopted and raised by the kindly Mrs. Tweed. In fact, he acted more like a house pet than a wild animal, which made Copper think Tod was just an odd-looking dog.

Copper belonged to Amos, who lived down the road from Mrs. Tweed's farm. Amos also had another dog named Chief, who he hoped would teach young Copper the ways of hunting. Amos was disappointed with Copper's lack of progress so far.

Whenever Tod came around, it was Chief who strained at his rope, while Copper stood by and did nothing. Thank goodness neither Amos nor Chief realized that Tod and Copper were friends. That would only have made matters worse.

"I wish Amos and Chief thought I was a good hunting dog," Copper told Tod one day. "I want them to be proud of me."

"Well, imagine what they'll say when you chase off a bear!" Tod replied.

"A bear?" Copper asked. "What's gotten into you?

"An idea, that's what!" answered Tod. "Yup, you're going to show them just what a great hunter you are—and I'm going to help you!"

That night, when Amos was asleep, the fox and the hound left a trail of berries leading from deep in the forest up to Amos's door.

Then Tod silently climbed up a stack of crates to the roof, and Copper hid behind a large rock. The pair waited, their hearts thumping in anticipation. Before too long, a big black bear emerged from the woods, stopping every few steps to gobble up the berries. When the bear reached the front door, Tod rolled a stick off the roof, just as he and Copper had planned. It hit the bear square on the head, and the huge creature let out a loud growl. The bear turned, dazed but unharmed, and ran back off into the woods.

Meanwhile, Amos was scrambling out of bed. "Come on, Chief!" he ordered. "There's something out there!"

As soon as the bear was gone for sure, Copper emerged from his hiding place and began to bark as loudly and fiercely as he could. But Amos was already at the door. "I don't believe it!" he cried, examining the bear prints in the mud. "Copper…can it be? Did you run off a bear all by yourself?"

Copper eagerly ran up to his master and wagged his tail while Amos patted him proudly on the head. Even old Chief was looking at the pup differently. "Maybe you'll make a fine hunting dog, after all," Amos said. Tod watched from his hiding place, happy to have helped his friend. He and Copper sure did make a great team!

Saved by the Cat!

Oliver was so happy living in his new home! There was plenty to eat and a soft pillow to sleep on, and best of all, a wonderful little girl named Jenny to care for him. Jenny was happy, too. Oliver was soft and cuddly, and he was lots of fun to play with. But there was one member of the household who was not so happy about this recent addition to the family, and that was Jenny's poodle, Georgette.

Until Oliver came, Georgette was Jenny's only pet. Now she had to share the little girl's love, and the poodle didn't like it one bit. Oliver knew Georgette wasn't fond of him, but he tried to win her over just the same. He shared his bowls of milk, and snuggled up to her in a friendly way whenever she lay down to take a nap. But the poodle just ignored him.

Then one day, when Winston went to collect the morning paper, Georgette and Oliver slipped out of the house. Oliver followed the butler back inside, but the poodle was left outside. She looked around in dismay.

37

"Maybe if I walk around to the back of the house and bark outside the kitchen window, Winston will hear me," she said to herself. But the minute she stepped onto the sidewalk, a terrible thing happened.

A truck pulled up to the curb and a man in uniform got out. "Just as I thought," said the dogcatcher, crouching to look at Georgette. "No tag. Well, little lady, I'm afraid you'll have to come with me." Then, as Oliver watched in horror, the man scooped up the poodle, loaded her into his truck, and drove away. Thinking quickly, Oliver hurried off to the old barge where his friend Dodger lived with a bunch of other dogs. After Oliver told them what had happened, Dodger came up with a plan. Soon the dogs were assembled on the sidewalk in front of the pound, barking and yelping at the top of their lungs. The front door flew open and the dogcatcher rushed out, but the gang raced in different directions—all except little Tito, who dashed inside and quickly found Georgette's cage. "Don't worry, I'll have you out of here in no time!" he promised as he set to work picking the lock. Within seconds, the poodle and the Chihuahua slipped out the back door. Then they met up with the rest of the group and headed back to the barge.

Georgette was so relieved to be free that she didn't mind that Oliver was there waiting. In fact, she hated to admit it, but his familiar face was a welcome sight. "Georgette! I'm so glad you're safe!" exclaimed the kitten. "Jenny is going to be so happy to see you!"

"Oliver's the one who got us to rescue you," Dodger pointed out.

That night, safe and sound at Jenny's house, an exhausted Georgette collapsed in her bed. Oliver quietly crept in and curled up beside her. This time, instead of pushing him away, the grateful poodle inched over and gave him a little more room. Cats weren't really all that bad once you broke them in, she thought.

Dumbo Leads the Way

Dumbo was so excited! He was appearing in his very first circus parade. He held on tight to his mother's tail and followed her down the street, amazed at all of the waving, smiling people. It made him feel important to be part of something that seemed to make others so happy. He daydreamed about the day when he might lead the spectacular procession. Lost in thought, Dumbo stumbled over his enormous ears. Soon a boy from the crowd began to taunt him. He pulled Dumbo's ears roughly and made fun of their huge size. When Dumbo's mother, Mrs. Jumbo, could stand it no longer, she lifted the boy up with her trunk.

"Help! Help!" the boy shrieked, even though Mrs. Jumbo was not hurting him. The boy fussed and kicked until Mrs. Jumbo

put him down on the sidewalk. That's when the other children gathered around the boy.

"Scaredy-cat!" teased a little girl.

"Boy, did you look silly!" laughed a boy.

"What a chicken!" called another. "Afraid of a dumb old elephant!"

The bully's cheeks grew red, and he stared at the pavement. His chin began to tremble, and he ran off down the street and hid in an alley. The others' hurtful remarks were still ringing in his ears, and soon he began to sob.

CLANK! CLANK! The boy looked up to see Mrs. Jumbo being led away in chains.

HONK! HONK! Then he heard what sounded like something quite large blowing its nose. He looked up and saw Dumbo. The baby elephant had gigantic tears rolling down his face, and his whole body shook with every sob. The boy realized that Dumbo was crying because they had taken his mother away.

He felt ashamed. He had just found out how terrible it was to be picked on. "I'm sorry for all the trouble I caused," he told the elephant. "I didn't think about your feelings. I guess

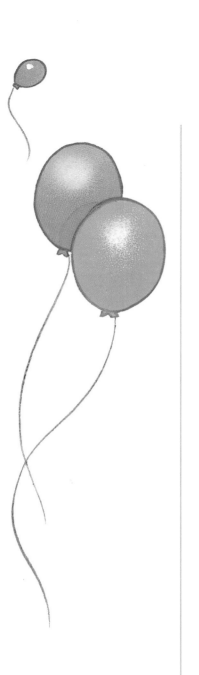

I wanted the other kids
to notice me. I didn't
mean the awful things I said."
The boy thought for a moment. "Why
don't we go back?" he suggested. "Maybe I can explain
to everyone that your mother had a good reason to act the way
she did. Then maybe they'll bring her back!"

Back on Main Street, the other children began to shout
and point at Dumbo.

"Hey, big ears!" they chanted. "Watch your step!"

The boy stood in front of his newfound friend.
"Stop teasing him! I'm sure you wouldn't like it if
someone made fun of you," he told them.
"Besides, his ears are perfect for him just
the way they are."

The children watched in awe as
Dumbo smiled and lifted the boy onto
his back. As the elephant marched
down the street, head held high, the
other children ran behind them,
clamoring for a ride. For the
moment, Dumbo felt like the
leader of the parade—and his
friend felt ten feet tall.

Cinderella's Uninvited Guests

It was almost too wonderful to believe. One day Cinderella was sweeping fireplaces and scrubbing floors, and the next she was engaged to a prince! Thank goodness the Grand Duke had asked her to try on the glass slipper that she lost at the ball, or the Prince might never have found his true love.

A lavish party was planned in the couple's honor. Within days, invitations were delivered to everyone in the kingdom—everyone except Cinderella's mean stepmother and two wicked stepsisters.

"There must be some mistake!" said Cinderella's stepmother to her daughters, Anastasia and Drizella. "We must attend! The most eligible princes from near and far will be there!"

That night, Anastasia and Drizella approached the palace gates with their mother. But when they could not present an invitation, one of the king's guards turned them away.

"And after all the time it took me to iron this gown," whined Anastasia. "Ever since Cinderella left, I feel like a maid!"

"You brilliant child!" exclaimed their mother. "You've just given me an idea!"

A short while later, Anastasia, Drizella, and their mother returned to the palace dressed as maids. With them they carried a large box containing all their party finery.

They confidently strode past the guard to the servants' entrance. But their triumph was soon destroyed by the Grand Duke, who stood scowling in the doorway. "You're late!" he bellowed. Then he handed them a long list of chores. "Get to work, and don't stop until you reach the end!" he added.

The three had no choice but to do as they were told. Finally, after they had completed their tasks, the exhausted trio changed into their gowns and slipped into the ballroom.

"Now, mingle," the mother instructed as she headed off to the buffet table. "And most of all, be charming!"

"I've got a better idea," said Drizella as she pulled Anastasia down to sit on a velvet love seat. "This is better than mingling. Now all those handsome young men will see us as they pass by."

And she was right. Soon two dashing princes from a neighboring kingdom approached. "Excuse me, ladies," said one gallantly. "We were wondering if you might honor us with the pleasure of a dance."

When there was no response, he peered closely. It was only then that he realized that both young women had fallen asleep with their eyes wide open! Suddenly Anastasia and Drizella shifted in their seats and began to snore. The princes hurried away in dismay. A little while later, Cinderella happened by and covered the two sisters with a shawl.

When Anastasia and Drizella woke at last, the ballroom was nearly empty. "So there you are!" cried the Grand Duke as he approached with a bucket and pail. "Time to clean up!"

"You know," said Anastasia to her sister, "these parties just aren't as much fun as they used to be!"

Timon's Snack Attack

It was a hot summer afternoon, and Timon hadn't done a single thing all day except sleep. He stretched and yawned and looked around for his two friends, Pumbaa and Simba. "I'll catch up with them later," he thought. "All this relaxing has given me an appetite. Time to grab some lunch."

He strolled through the jungle whistling, turning over logs and looking under rocks for a nice, juicy bug or two. Then, suddenly, he spied something unusual sitting peacefully among the green leaves of a bush. "My, my, what have we here?" the little meerkat wondered, his hopes rising.

Timon had never seen a bug like this before. It was round and black and had very, very long antennae sticking out on both sides of it. But the creature ducked into the bush, leaving Timon empty-handed.

Just then Pumbaa and Simba walked up behind their friend. "What are you doing?" Simba asked.

"Beating around the bush," replied Timon, shaking the plant's branches. "There's a tasty new insect hiding in there."

"Come out, little bug!" Pumbaa called encouragingly.

Timon just rolled his eyes and peered into the leaves. Suddenly he heard a strange growling sound. "What was that?" he asked nervously.

"My stomach, I'll bet!" giggled Simba. "Talking about food makes me hungry."

"Time to let my fingers do the walking!" announced Timon. He stood up purposefully and plunged his hand into the bush. "Oh! I think I found it. Wow, it sure is cold and wet!"

His words were answered by a YOWL! so sudden it made all three friends jump.

"Gee, Simba," Pumbaa said. "You really are hungry."

"It wasn't me that time—honest," Simba replied.

Now the bush began to move and shake, and the cold, wet thing Timon had found started to push against his paw. And it kept right on pushing until it poked through the leaves for all to see.

"Look, guys!" Timon said triumphantly. "It's the brand-new snack I was telling you about!"

"Funny, it looks just like a nose," mused Pumbaa. "With whiskers."

Timon turned to his buddy. "Don't be ridiculous!" he said, trying to pull the bug off the leaf.

"Uh-oh," said Simba, pointing behind Timon's back.

Timon looked over his shoulder and discovered that his bug wasn't really a bug at all. It was a cheetah's nose—with a cheetah cub attached.

"Nice kitty," said Timon, backing away as the drowsy cub regarded him with curiosity. "Could we get you some warm milk? If you slept more, you could get rid of those circles under your eyes."

Simba jabbed him. "Those aren't circles, they're spots," he whispered.

But the trio had nothing to fear, for the cub soon turned his back, curled up under the bush, and went back to his nap.

Timon sank against a tree while Pumbaa and Simba tried hard not to laugh. "New rules!" he announced. "From now on, we're vegetarians!"

"Watch" Dogs

Roger, Anita, Perdita, and Pongo loved taking walks together—especially with Pongo and Perdita's fifteen Dalmatian puppies. One afternoon, as the foursome prepared for their daily stroll, Roger called out, "C'mon, everyone—time to go!"

Not a single puppy came running out. "That's odd," Perdita said to Pongo, growing concerned. "I think we'd better go see what they're up to." When they walked past the living room, they found their entire brood in front of the television set. The pups sat motionless in the flickering light, watching the adventures of their hero, a brave dog named Thunderbolt.

"Children, do you want to go for a walk?" Perdita asked.

"Not now, Mom," Lucky replied, glancing reluctantly away from the screen. "We'll miss the best part!"

Later that day, Nanny prepared the puppies' supper and placed their bowls in a row on the kitchen floor. But when she rang the dinner bell, nothing happened.

Just then Anita came through the door. "Unless you plan on making those TV dinners," she said, "I don't think you'll be seeing the puppies this evening."

"Thunderbolt again?" asked Nanny. "Why, all those youngsters seem to do these days is watch the telly."

And so it went for the next several days until Pongo and Perdita decided that, from now on, the pups would only be allowed to watch one hour of TV a day. But before they had a chance to break the news, Lucky came bursting into the kitchen.

"The set's broken!" he wailed. "We'll miss the show!"

Pongo and Perdita followed him into the living room, where Roger was peering into the back of the set. "I'm afraid I'm going to have to call a repairman," he said.

"Oh, no!" cried Rolly. "What are we going to do until then?"

"Yeah," added Patch. "Compared to watching Thunderbolt, everything else is boring."

"It's a beautiful day," said Perdita, looking out the window. "Why don't you go outside and play?"

"Do we have to?" Lucky groaned.

"Yes! Go on, now," she insisted.

All fifteen puppies reluctantly filed out the back door and headed for the grassy area in the square.

"I'll bet Thunderbolt never plays catch," Patch said, absent-mindedly pushing a rubber ball with his nose.

"Never," Rolly replied. "He's too busy doing exciting stuff. Remember how he found some buried treasure?"

"Yeah!" said Patch. "Let's try to find some!"

"Where should we start?" Lucky asked.

"How about right here?" Rolly exclaimed. And so the puppies began searching in the bushes, under trees, in the flower beds, under benches, and anywhere else they could think of.

"Look what I found!" cried Patch, holding up an old chewed slipper. Then Rolly found a tasty candy wrapper, and Lucky discovered a squeaky toy they had lost a long time ago.

After a while Pongo came outside. "All right, the TV is fixed now. But remember, you can only watch for an hour!" he reminded them.

"Later, Dad!" called Patch. "Watching adventures on TV is fun, but having them is even better!"

Mowgli the Bear Tamer

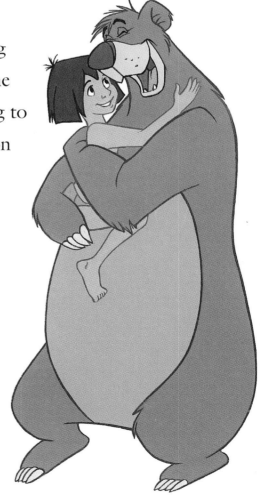

Mowgli the Man-cub and Baloo the bear were best friends. They loved wandering through the jungle together, doing whatever they felt like doing whenever they felt like doing it. But one day it was time for Mowgli to give up his carefree ways and go to live in the Man-village.

Baloo missed Mowgli very much, and wondered how Mowgli was getting along in his new home. "I know," said Baloo to himself. "I'll just pay the little Man-cub a visit."

The happy bear set off for the Man-village, stopping frequently to munch on yummy snacks. When at last he arrived, he stood on the outskirts of the village, hoping to catch sight of his old friend. Sure enough, Mowgli soon came outside the compound to get some water from the stream. As he bent down to fill his pot, he saw Baloo's reflection in the rippling water. "Baloo!" Mowgli almost shouted, but then he remembered the villagers just beyond. Instead he just smiled and jumped into his old friend's arms, and the two gave each other a great big bear hug.

"I'm so happy to see you," Mowgli whispered.

"What are you doing here?"

"Just checking up on my old pal," Baloo told him. "So how are they treating you around here?"

"It took a while to get used to living with people," Mowgli replied. "But I like it fine now. There's just one thing."

"What's that?" Baloo asked, dangling his feet in the stream.

"Well, nobody believes me when I tell them about you and Bagheera," Mowgli explained. "They say a mere boy could never have traveled in the company of fierce creatures such as bears and panthers."

"Then we'll just have to show 'em they're wrong," Baloo cried, and together the two came up with a plan.

That night at dusk, Baloo entered the village, making as much noise as he could. He tried to look menacing, baring his teeth and swiping at the air with his sharp claws. Terrified, the women and children ran for cover while the men rushed to fetch their weapons.

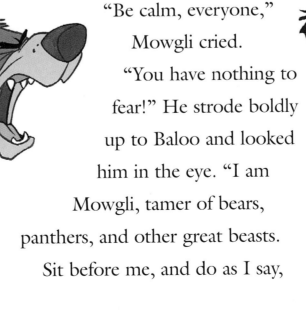

"Be calm, everyone," Mowgli cried.

"You have nothing to fear!" He strode boldly up to Baloo and looked him in the eye. "I am Mowgli, tamer of bears, panthers, and other great beasts. Sit before me, and do as I say, for I am your master." At this, Baloo plunked himself on the ground and stared straight ahead as if in a trance.

"I command you to bring three pots of water from the stream!" Mowgli said in his most grown-up voice. Baloo did as he was told, returning with one pot in each paw, and the other balanced on his head. The villagers stared in disbelief.

"Now go over to that tree and gather the bananas that have fallen beneath it!" ordered Mowgli. Baloo picked up a nearby basket, and when he returned it was brimming with fruit.

Astonished, the head of the village asked, "What else can you make a wild animal do?"

"Well," replied Mowgli slowly, "I can make him...dance!"

Baloo gave Mowgli a wink and grabbed his hand. Together they did a wild dance, while the villagers—getting into the spirit of things now—played drums and horns to accompany them.

Finally, the pair collapsed in an exhausted heap while the villagers gathered for a closer look. Mowgli could see that Baloo had a grin coming on, and decided to end their prank while they still could.

"Mowgli commands you to return to the jungle!" the Man-cub said sternly. Baloo gave his friend another little wink, then walked out of the village, grabbing a few bunches of bananas from the basket.

Putting on a performance like that made a bear hungry!

When it was safe, Baloo turned and glanced back at the village. But he needn't have worried. All eyes were on Mowgli as his neighbors paraded him around the village on a makeshift throne. "Hail to Mowgli, tamer of beasts!" Baloo could hear the people shout. He just smiled and popped another banana in his mouth. How strange these Man-creatures could be!